MEET ALL THESE FRIENDS IN BUZZ BOOKS:

Thomas the Tank Engine
The Animals of Farthing Wood
Biker Mice From Mars
James Bond Junior
Fireman Sam
Joshua Jones
Rupert
Babar

First published in Great Britain 1994 by Buzz Books,
an imprint of Reed Children's Books
Michelin House, 81 Fulham Road, London SW3 6RB
and Auckland, Melbourne, Singapore and Toronto

ISBN 1 85591 449 2

Printed in Italy by Olivotto

Peace

Story by Colin Dann
Text by Mary Risk
Illustrations by The County Studio

Times had been hard for Fox's cub, Bold.
When he first ran away from White Deer
Park, he had been healthy and strong,
full of hope and confidence.

"I'll make my own way in the world,"
he had thought. "I don't need my father
to tell me what to do."

But Bold had not understood the
dangers that lay in wait for him outside
the park.

A gamekeeper's trap had damaged his
eyes and a hunter's gun had crippled his
hind leg. He was weak and ill, struggling
to survive.

Luckily, Bold had made good friends.
Crow often brought him food and
Whisper became his mate.

Now Whisper was expecting Bold's cubs.

"I want them to be born in White Deer Park," she said to Bold.

Bold sighed heavily. "But I've sworn never to go back," he replied.

"Please," said Whisper, nuzzling him. "I want our cubs to grow up in safety with the rest of your family."

So Bold and Whisper set out on the
long journey to the park. But Bold was
weak. He couldn't hunt, and soon he
was hungry and exhausted.

"We're nearly there. Just keep going a
little longer," coaxed Whisper.

"I'm sorry, Whisper," said Bold softly.
"I can't go any further."

"Wait here," said Whisper, looking at him anxiously. "I'll go and hunt for food."

"Thank your lucky stars you've got such a good mate," cawed someone overhead.

Bold looked up.

"Crow!" he said. "You followed us!"

"Of course I did!" cawed Crow.

"That was kind of you." Painfully, Bold dragged himself under a bush. "I'll die here. Whisper will have to go on alone..."

"Caw! Don't give up yet," said Crow.

"Don't tell Whisper where I am," begged Bold, his voice weak. "I can't bear to say goodbye to her."

Whisper returned with food for Bold.

"Bold!" she called. "Where are you?"

"Caw! Caw!" said Crow.

Whisper looked up at him.

"Where's Bold?" she asked. "He was here earlier. Have you seen him?"

"Caw," said Crow again.

Whisper searched the meadow for Bold.
She knew he couldn't have gone far, but
Bold lay quietly under the bush and
Whisper didn't find him.

"He's gone away to die," she thought
sadly. "I shall have to go on alone. The
cubs must be born in safety!"

Bold heard her slowly walk away.

"Goodbye, dear Whisper," he
murmured.

In White Deer Park, Bold's sister, Charmer, went out to meet Ranger. Though he was Scarface's son, Ranger didn't agree with the quarrel between the Farthing Wood foxes and the blue foxes.

"Kee!" called Kestrel from overhead. "A new fox has entered the park! She's coming your way!"

Whisper approached.

"Please," she said, "where can I find the Farthing Wood Fox? I'm Bold's mate."

"Bold? Where is he? Is he coming home?" asked Charmer eagerly.

"No," said Whisper. "He'll never come home now."

Charmer took Whisper to see Fox
and Vixen.

"Bold's mate!" said Vixen. "How
wonderful! Where is Bold, my dear?"

Whisper bowed her head sadly.

"I left him just outside the park," she
said. "I think — I think he's dying."

"We'll go at once," said Fox.

"Oh, Bold, my foolish son!" sighed
Vixen. "Why ever did you run away?"

"Our friend, Crow, might know where
Bold is," said Whisper. "But I'll stay here,
if I may. I've a feeling Bold has already
said goodbye to me."

"Of course," Vixen replied, and she
bounded away with Fox at her heels.

Crow saw Fox and Vixen coming.

"Your son is here," he told them.

Fox and Vixen peered beneath the bush.

Bold struggled to open his eyes.

"Mother? Father?" he said weakly. "Is that you?"

"Yes, Bold," said Vixen, "we're here."

"My mate Whisper...is on her way to White Deer Park..." began Bold.

"We've seen her," said Fox. "Whisper and the new cubs will be safe with us."

"Thanks, Father," sighed Bold.

"Son," said Fox, "I'm sorry I was so hard on you. I am proud of you."

Bold managed a small smile, then his eyes gently closed.

Death hung over White Deer Park that day. Adder had a score to settle with Scarface, the leader of the blue foxes. The quarrel had to stop.

Adder lay in wait in a clump of reeds near the stream.

Sure enough, Scarface arrived. He had a drink, then plunged into the stream for a swim.

"Here isss my chance," hissed Adder.

She slipped into the water after Scarface and sank her fangs into his hind leg.

Scarface howled in pain. He struggled out of the water and onto the bank.

"Adder," he snarled, "you've killed me!"

"It wasss high time," hissed Adder.

"My son will avenge my death. The feud goes on!" said Scarface, then he collapsed.

Adder slid away towards the pond.

"Hello, matey!" said Toad.

"The park isss sssafe now," Adder
announced. "Ssscarface is dead."

The word spread quickly among the
Farthing Wood animals.

"This calls for a party!" cackled Weasel.

While the other animals celebrated the death of their enemy, Fox and Vixen were grieving for Bold.

"We mustn't celebrate the loss of a life, even after the trouble Scarface caused," Fox told his friends. "There are always some left behind who will mourn."

Fox was right.

"I know he was a scoundrel," Ranger said to Charmer, "but Scarface was my father, and I loved him in my own way."

"I suppose he would have wanted you to avenge his death," said Charmer.

"Yes, I'm sure that's what he would have wanted," Ranger replied. "But the feud must stop."

"Let's go and tell Father!" said Charmer.

Ranger smiled. "Maybe now he'll accept me as your mate."

Fox and Vixen were comforting Whisper when Charmer and Ranger ran up.

"The quarrel is over!" called Charmer.

Fox looked at Ranger. "Is this true?"

"Yes, the feud is truly over," Ranger declared. "On my honour."

"Some good news at last," said Fox.

"Fox," said Ranger, "Charmer and I would like to be mates."

Fox smiled. "Perhaps one day your cubs and Bold's cubs will play together," he said, "and we'll all live in peace."